Joan —

Merry Christmas 1998!

Love,

Helyn

TO WHOM THE ANGEL SPOKE

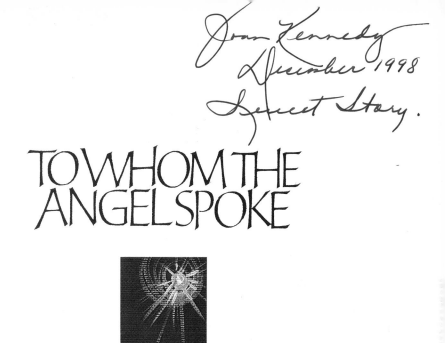

A Story of the Christmas

Terry Kay

Illustrated by Eileen Blyth

PEACHTREE PUBLISHERS, LTD.
Atlanta

PEACHTREE PUBLISHERS, LTD.
494 Armour Circle, NE / Atlanta, GA 30324

Text © 1991 Terry Kay
Illustrations © 1991 Eileen Blyth

Printed in MEXICO.
Printed and bound by Impresora Donneco Internacional S.A. de C.V.
R .R. Donnelley & Sons Co., Division Reynosa/McAllen
Jackets printed by Stein Printing Company, Atlanta, Georgia
Color separations by Magna Graphic South, Orlando, Florida

1st printing [1991]

Designed by Candace J. Magee
Illustrations rendered in acrylic on paper by Eileen Blyth
Composed in Garamond Light Condensed and Light Condensed Italic
by Kathryn D. Mothershed
Title handlettered by Joey Hannaford

Library of Congress Cataloging-in-Publication Data

Kay, Terry.
    To whom the angel spoke / Terry Kay.
      p. cm.
    ISBN 1-56145-034-0
      1. Jesus Christ--Nativity. 2. Shepherds in the Bible. I. Title.
    BT315.2.K33 1991
    232.92'2--dc20   91-16663
                                          CIP

For Brooks and Jordan,
who keep the stories alive.

With my love,
Papa

Author's Note

I wrote the first version of this story almost 20 years ago, as a reading. I still think of it that way, because I believe there are some stories that need to be said aloud. I want **TO WHOM THE ANGEL SPOKE** to be one of them.

In this version, I have elected to use scripture from the King James version of the Bible. It is a personal preference, having absolutely nothing to do with theology, but everything to do with poetry.

TO WHOM THE ANGEL SPOKE

nce upon a time,
there were three shepherds
who lived together to keep
watch over their sheep.

Oh, there may have been more than three
of them, but that doesn't matter. Three is a
good number. Not too few. Not too many.

What does matter is that the three shepherds were good at their work, and their work was not easy. They had to protect their flocks from wild animals, and they had to know where to find fields of deep, thick grass and pools of clean, clear water. They had to know when their sheep were restless and wanted to move about, or when they wanted to rest.

Certainly, the three shepherds knew about sheep.

Still, as people, living together, they were different.

One shepherd was tall.

Another shepherd was short.

The third shepherd was neither tall nor short.
He looked short when he stood beside the tall
shepherd and tall when he stood beside the
short shepherd.

He was in-between. Medium.

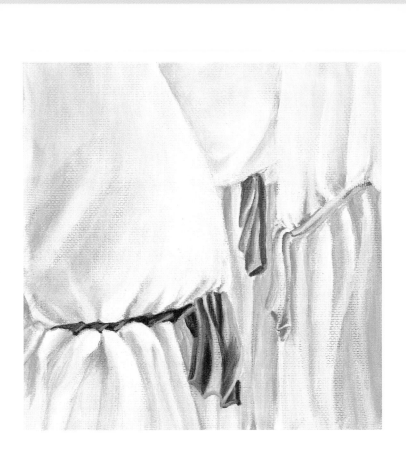

One shepherd was fat.

Another shepherd was thin.

The third shepherd was neither fat nor thin. He looked fat when he stood beside the thin shepherd and thin when he stood beside the fat shepherd.

He was in-between. Medium.

One shepherd was black.

Another shepherd was white.

The third shepherd was neither black nor white. His skin was the color of rich bronze, and when he stood beside the black shepherd, he looked curiously pale, but when he stood beside the white shepherd, he looked curiously dark. It was very curious how he looked when he stood between both his friends at the same time — a kind of pale-dark, dark-pale.

You see, he was, well, in-between. Medium.

The three shepherds were different, as all people, everywhere, are different.

ecause they were shepherds, they would spend much of their time sitting and relaxing, watching as their sheep huddled in twos and threes and fours to graze from the grass.

As they sat and relaxed, the shepherds would sometimes sing songs they knew — different songs, often at the same time — and the sheep would look at them with puzzled faces as if to say, "What strange men are these shepherds who watch over us."

Sometimes, when they were not singing, they would grumble and argue among themselves.

"It is!" one shepherd would say.

"It is not!" another shepherd would reply.

"I don't know. If it is, it is. If it is not, it is not," the third shepherd would suggest.

"Well, I say it is."
"And I say it is not."
"And I don't know."

The three shepherds loved to argue — about anything.

And if they were not singing or arguing or polishing the crooks of their long shepherd's sticks, they would lie quietly in the spongy quilts of grass and listen to the sheep and imagine the sheep were speaking to them in an unknown language, telling them secrets no one had ever heard. Or they would listen to the wind whistle as it dipped and soared through the hills.

One shepherd said the wind made him lonely.
He thought a man should have a home and
not wander like a nomad through the hills.

"I don't like it, being out here," he complained.
"Sleeping on the grass, like sheep. A person should
have a place to go to at nighttime. He should have
a table to sit at when eating his food. He should
have a bed — a warm bed on cold nights."

Another shepherd said the wind made him restless. He thought he should have been a world traveller. Perhaps a trader. Someone who carried cloth to the seas and returned with spices from the city.

"Ah, that would have been a wonderful life," he said, dreamily. "To see the great cities of the world, to travel the great roads, to meet the great people in great places. That's better than staying in the hills, looking at sheep day after day."

The third shepherd — the in-between, medium one — said he didn't really think about the wind. It was part of being a shepherd, and, after all, that's what he was: a shepherd.

"Sometimes I would like to have a home and a table and a bed," he said to his friends. "Sometimes I would like to travel to the great cities on the great roads and meet the great people, but most of the time, it doesn't matter. I'm a shepherd. I don't mind being here in the hills."

They were very different, these three men who were shepherds.

One shepherd had been complaining about the new tax that the king, whose name was Herod, had demanded from the people.

"He's nothing but a money-grabber," he shouted loudly from the hills — knowing no one except the other two shepherds could hear him. "Why can't he pick on the rich? Bah! I'll not pay! He's a madman who should be made to live with swine. I'll not pay, I tell you. Taxes are high enough. Let them try to find me here in the hills! Let them send their soldiers. I won't pay!"

Another shepherd disagreed.

"We should pay," he argued. "Look how King Herod keeps away our enemies. True, he may be a pompous old man, but still he gives us something in return. All of that costs money. Soldiers can't feed on grass, like sheep. They can't fight faraway wars with sticks and stones. They need weapons. I don't mind paying. And if I had a home, I'd pay even more than they ask."

"Bah!" his companion roared. "He oppresses our people. We bow before him like dogs whining before their masters for bread crumbs. If I could travel over the world, to the great cities, I am sure I would find kings who do not oppress their people."

The third shepherd said he didn't care one way or the other. He didn't want to pay the tax, but he would if he had to.

His attitude was — well, in-between.

"I know so little about kings and soldiers and faraway wars," he confessed.

The only thing the third shepherd was curious about, was the constant caravan of people going into the small town of Bethlehem to pay the tax of Herod.

"I did not know so many had moved away," he said quietly. "I wonder if any of them are old friends. Perhaps I played with some of them as a boy. I wonder if I would remember any of them. It's been such a long time since I was a boy."

He smiled softly and added, "I remember playing hide-and-seek. I could hide in such places that no one could find me."

One of the other shepherds laughed.

"So that's where your sheep learned their hiding tricks," he said.

And, so, the three men who were shepherds
sat on the top of a hill overlooking Bethlehem
and watched the faraway, thin line of people
moving slowly along a rough, dusty road
toward the town.

"Fools!" yelled the angry shepherd, jabbing his shepherd's crook into the ground. "You're wasting your money on a tyrant."

"Faithful!" his friend called out, laughing and making fun of the first shepherd. "Be glad you have kings and soldiers to watch over you."

"I wish I were closer, so I might see who they are," sighed the third shepherd — the in-between one — as he gazed at the little haze of dust puffed up by the slow feet of men and animals.

Oh, yes, they were very, very different, the three men who were shepherds.

veryone who lived back then — back in the time of the three shepherds — remembered the night.

Sunset opened in a splatter of color — orange and red and purple. Slender streams of light reaching out from the palm of the sun, reaching out high and long to catch something in their bright fingers. Trees. Hills. The buildings of Bethlehem. Something. Anything.

The three shepherds marveled at the sunset. They stood, side by side — the in-between shepherd standing in-between the tall shepherd and the short shepherd — and they cupped their hands over their eyes to shade out the glare. The light settled over them and threw their shadows — tall, in-between, short shadows — against the mountain.

"Beautiful!" said one shepherd.

"Magnificent!" said another shepherd.

"Wonderful!" said the third shepherd.

For one rare moment, the three had agreed on something.

Even the sheep, which usually had little concern for such things, looked at the sunset. Some of them bleated. All of them looked.

And then the sunset disappeared and stars began to pop out against the blot of darkness. The stars sparkled and flamed and seemed to dance with brightness.

"I see bad weather in this night," said one of the shepherds, as he prepared to raise a tent.

"I think it is a good omen," said another shepherd. "I think we will have days of good grazing, valleys of thick grass and flowing streams of water."

"I do not know," said the third shepherd. "If it is not one, perhaps it will be the other."

The brightness kept the shepherds awake.

One was afraid.
Another was fascinated.
The third was curious.

And the sheep were restless.

"I think this is strange," said the black shepherd
— or it might have been the white shepherd,
or even the bronze shepherd; anyway, one of
them said it. "I think above us is the brightest
star the heavens ever held."

His friends nodded.

"Yes," said one.

"Quite so," said the other.

Again, the three shepherds had agreed on
something.

The star above them glittered like a brilliant, giant jewel turning with the wind. It caught the light of the moon and the other stars and threw the light toward earth, toward Bethlehem.

The three shepherds whispered in awe, each saying the same thing:

"Look . . ."
". . . Look."
". . . Look."

And as they were watching the star pour down its golden light upon Bethlehem and the hills around Bethlehem, the three shepherds heard something that sounded like a voice — words from the throat of the wind, rushing up from a distant valley, sliding over the lap of the hills in a whistling cry like the gathering of a sudden storm.

"What was that?" cried one of the shepherds.

"A voice. I know it. A — a windvoice," muttered the second shepherd.

"Yes, I heard it, too," whispered the third shepherd. "It — it said something like — like, *'Fear not.'*"

"Yes, yes, that was it," the first shepherd agreed. "*'Fear not.'* But why am I so afraid?"

The three shepherds moved closer together,
huddling like their sheep, and listened.

They heard the rushing sound of the windvoice again — mightier than before — and the light of the star rolled over them, and the three shepherds fell to the ground, terribly frightened. They threw their cloaks over their faces, trying to hide from the light and the windvoice.

The fat shepherd began mumbling prayers learned long ago, as a child.

The thin shepherd began singing a psalm of David taught to him by his mother.

The third shepherd — who was neither fat nor thin — began chanting praises he had heard from travellers.

And then the windvoice became loud and clear.
It said again:

*"Fear not: for, behold, I bring you good tidings
of great joy, which shall be to all people."*

The three shepherds hugged each other in fear.

"Oh, what is happening?" they cried, trembling
so hard they were bumping heads.

And again the voice surrounded them:

"For unto you is born this day in the City of David a Saviour, which is Christ the Lord. And this shall be a sign unto you: Ye shall find the Babe wrapped in swaddling clothes, lying in a manger."

Then, out of the heavens, the shepherds heard other voices — voices that exploded and echoed throughout the hills:

"Glory to God in the highest, and on earth peace, good will toward men."

And then the voices were gone, leaving a silence as still as morning, untouched and clean. The three shepherds pulled off their cloaks from over their faces and looked at one another.

"How could this be?" whispered one.

"I do not know," said another. "How can voices come out of the wind? Does the wind know how to speak?"

"But it did," said the third. "It was the voice of the Lord. It had to be. Did we not hear the words?"

The other shepherds agreed:
"Yes."
"Yes."

The three shepherds sat and listened to the silence and stared at the star burning in the sky above them.

"It brings all of the light of the other stars to it," said one shepherd.

"I think it is the sun, which has broken apart," guessed another shepherd.

"Why did its light fall on us?" asked the third shepherd.

Then one of them said, "Let us go now even unto Bethlehem, and see this thing which is come to pass, which the Lord hath made known unto us."

"Yes, I agree," said another of the shepherds.

"Yes, let us go," said the third shepherd.

And, so, the three shepherds went into Bethlehem, following the bright path of the brightest star above them, and they came to a place where the child who would be named Jesus lay, wrapped in swaddling clothes as the windvoice had promised.

One by one, they bowed quietly before the child, and then each went away to tell a different story of what had happened, because the three shepherds — those to whom the angel spoke — were different, as all people, everywhere, are different.

Yet, they heard a voice one night, and because they believed what the voice told them, they were alike.

And again that voice speaks. To all who are different, but are seekers and askers and believers, that voice is heard always at the Christmas. It says, as it said to the three shepherds:

"For unto you is born this day in the City of David a Saviour, which is Christ the Lord."

Amen. Amen.

About the Author

Terry Kay is a former journalist and an award-winning novelist and screenwriter. His books include THE YEAR THE LIGHTS CAME ON (1976); AFTER ELI (1981) for which he won the Georgia Author of the Year Award; DARK THIRTY (1984); and the acclaimed TO DANCE WITH THE WHITE DOG (1990). AFTER ELI, DARK THIRTY and TO DANCE WITH THE WHITE DOG have all been optioned for film. He won an Emmy Award for his screenplay for "Run Down the Rabbit." A contributing editor to *Atlanta* Magazine, Kay lives in Lilburn, Georgia.